Lonely Strangers

Elie Victor

Lonely Strangers

Olympia Publishers
London

www.olympiapublishers.com
OLYMPIA PAPERBACK EDITION

A CIP catalogue record for this title is
available from the British Library.

ISBN: 978-1-83543-083-5

This is a work of fiction.
Names, characters, places and incidents originate from the writer's
imagination. Any resemblance to actual persons, living or dead, is
purely coincidental.

First Published in 2024

Olympia Publishers
Tallis House
2 Tallis Street
London
EC4Y 0AB

Printed in Great Britain

Dedication

This book is dedicated to the many people who have supported and believed in me, without whom I would not be the person, I am today.

The Undertaker

"Did I ever tell you about that weird story I heard once from my friend. Friend of my dad actually. The story about that undertaker?"

My mind was already starting to feel foggy and my body was slowly falling asleep, resting on the counter.

I never was a great conversationalist, but my friend Oliver somehow always had interesting, funny or awkward stories to tell when we met for drinks. We met every Friday in our favourite pub, an old-fashion pub in East London. It was never busy, the lights were dim and the drinks were cheaper than in most pubs. It was nothing special but it was where we always went after a long boring week, and enjoyed a few glasses of liquor while we caught up. We never talked about our work or complained about how uninteresting they were, because we always found something else to talk about, and I always looked forward to his stories. As I mentioned already, he usually spoke more and I listened.

"An undertaker? I don't remember that one," I said, barely raising my head from the counter.

Oliver smiled.

"It actually is a rather curious one, I think you'll like it. You like these kind of stories."

After five days of the week, the weight of daily life troubles and three glasses of liquor, it did not take much more than Oliver's promise of a good story to captivate me.

I raised from the counter, put my elbows on it and rested my head on my hands. Then I stared at him, waiting for him to start.

He cleared his throat and took on a sort-of dramatic tone.

"So, basically." Oliver paused, finished his glass of Hibiki mid-sentence. "I don't remember all the details, but it goes like this."

*

Josiah had always had a very simple vision of his work. No matter how closely related he was to death, he never thought about it more, or in a different way than anyone else. Josiah dug holes in the ground, watched people dressed in black mourn from afar, then put back the dirt he had dug, covering the casket of someone he did not know. And to him, that is all there was to it.

Death was, part of life, true, but it was his job. He did not fear it, he did not spend hours pondering about it. He knew that one day it would come for him, and someone else would do for him, what he did once in a while for others. Nothing more nothing less.

It was one of these days, or rather evenings, he was lazily standing under the big tree in the cemetery, watching a small group of people gathered, to fair goodbyes to their lost relative, one last time. Josiah was just waiting for the pastor to finish his sermon, so people could leave. Then he would do his job like he had done hundreds of times before.

After everyone was gone, Josiah walked to the hole in the ground, covered it with dirt again, and soon enough, he was done. He left the cemetery after a good day's work.

It was rather still early and he had nothing better to do, so he decided to go to his usual pub where his acquaintances met up.

Josiah thought of them as acquaintances, none of them were close enough to be considered friends. He did not mind that much, not having real close friends. All he cared about was doing his job, paying a visit to his mother from time to time, to make sure that even living on her own, she was doing well, and sometimes enjoy a beer or two with people he got along with. He was still young, and one day he would simply leave his small hometown and start a different life somewhere else. Maybe find another job. That was only a small idea, far back in his mind. For now, his situation satisfied him.

He left the pub a few hours after the sun had gone down, and slowly walked back to his house. The air was cold but the drinks had warmed his body, so he took his time walking, enjoying the night life of the town. The lights in the streets, the sound coming from the busy restaurants and bars, people talking and laughing, enjoying the last night of their well-deserved rest days.

Yes, Josiah thought, *this life satisfies me.*

That night however, sleep was long to come. And he did not know why. It was late now, he was feeling tired from the digging and the drinking. But he could not sleep.

Resigned, Josiah got up and switched the lights on, before sitting at his desk in the small bedroom.

When he had free time, which he had lots of, Josiah liked to write. Mainly he wrote in a journal, where he kept track of his activities, thoughts and the likes. There was nothing especially exciting about his daily life to write about mind you, but it was something he enjoyed doing. And he hoped trying to write tonight would help him find sleep. So, he wrote.

Today, I had to bury someone again. I believe it is the sixth person this month. It was Mrs Dunham, the old lady mother used to buy the newspaper from. She had always been nice to me when

9

I was younger, but I realise now I did not know much about her, except that she sold newspapers.

I have been digging and covering holes in the same town for almost five years now. Time flies.

Josiah stopped and read what he had written so far, with immense focus. He did not know what else to add, there was really so much to say about Mrs Dunham, and now that he had covered her casket, there would never be anything else to say about her. So he changed the subject and continued to write.

At the pub, the boys were all talking about how small and boring the town is and how they cannot wait to leave. I suppose I agree, but I still do not know what I am going to do. I cannot leave until Mother dies. And even then I do not know where I could go. But I will leave when I do not enjoy life here any more.

Once again Josiah stopped writing and went over his freshly inked page again. Still, he did not feel like sleep would come easily. It was Sunday night, and Josiah would probably have no work to do until the next Sunday. Everyone was buried on Sundays in this town. Which meant that sleeping tonight was not mandatory for him, if he slept all of Monday morning no one would come complaining about it to him.

For the first time in a long time, Josiah felt frustration. He realised that there was really not much to do apart from digging holes every Sunday and resting every other day. He could write, read, go for walks and meet the people in the pub. But now he felt like maybe this life was not satisfying him as much as he had convinced himself it did.

This new feeling, this strange feeling of wanting something more, this strange feeling that somehow his life was not really his or that, perhaps, it was not really life, took him by surprise. This new feeling, he did not know how to cope with. So he went out again, to get some fresh air, clear his mind and walk around town. *It will pass, I will feel better tomorrow,* he thought. But for some reason tomorrow was not something he was looking forward to all of a sudden.

After making sure his door was locked, Josiah took a stroll around, with no particular destination, not even minding where his feet were leading him to.

The air outside had become even colder, but he did not mind. Being late, the noise had become much more muffled, as most people had gone home and most places had started closing.

"Hey, mister."

Josiah stopped walking. An old man slowly walked towards him. He was wearing a coat, but it was in very bad shape and probably did not provide much resistance to this cold night. Josiah instantly recognised him. He was a poor homeless man, the only one in the town. This old man, everyone who knew him tried to help him as they could, but there was only so much they could do.

"Sorry, lad, I wish I had something to give you but I truly don't."

"Oh, I don't want anything from you." The old man was visibly drunk, but he was smiling at Josiah. "I just felt like talking to someone for a bit."

Again Josiah remembered he had nothing better to do, but there was really nothing to talk about, and they just stood in front of each other without saying a word.

Then the old man broke the silence.

"I cannot believe they buried Mrs Dunham, you know. A sweet lady she was. Very sweet."

Josiah nodded. The old man knew more about her than he ever would apparently.

"I know, I was glad to see she had people close to her. Lots of people came to her funeral."

The old man looked at him again.

"Can you believe I outlived her? Who would have thought? It's a strange world we live in, mister. A strange world, indeed."

Josiah had never thought the world was a strange place before. Until now, the world had been many things: cold, boring, frustrating, sad. But never had it been strange. Josiah was not even sure he could explain why or how the world had suddenly become strange. Nevertheless, he replied with a very casual, "I guess so." And started walking again after saying goodbye to the old man.

After a few more minutes of walking, Josiah ended up in front if the cemetery gate. It was dark as no lamppost illuminated the grave at night. It was not really the place people went to at night. But for some reason, he decided to go in the graveyard and just loiter there for a while. It was a quiet, peaceful place. Tonight, the graveyard gave him an appeasing feeling he had never felt before. Or maybe he had never noticed. It almost felt like it was his place. Where he should be. It felt good and his mind stopped feeling troubled.

A crow came to his feet, as Josiah was passing by the graves of people he had never known, but had most definitely buried. The crow seemed to be welcoming in this haven that now felt more like home than his bedroom ever had.

Josiah did not know why, but he was sure the crow was trying to show him a way. Every time it flew farther from him, the crow stopped and waited, patiently, for him to follow it. And so he did. The crow wanted to show Josiah something.

He kept following the crow until it stopped on one grave, a small grave, discreet, hidden amongst dozens others, a grave no one would pay particular attention to. But there was something special about the grave. No-one else could know, but that was just the way it was. The hole had not been covered. This seemed impossible to Josiah as he knew he was the only undertaker of the town, and he would know if he had forgotten to cover a hole. But there it was. The casket in the hole was not covered. The crow was standing on the casket and had its dark eyes fixed on Josiah. And like old friends, who do not need to speak any more, Josiah knew what the crow wanted him to do. Josiah opened the casket. What he found inside did not disgust him, did not surprise him either. He was feeling serene and at peace as he never had before, and nothing would change how he we was feeling that night. In the casket laid a spitting image of himself. Josiah, the undertaker, was lying down inside a casket, and his reflection was staring back at him from above. Josiah said farewell to the crow and finally found the deep, unperturbed sleep he had been looking for that night.

On Sunday, a small grave, discreet, hidden amongst dozens others, a grave no one would pay particular attention to, was made. And after the few people had gathered and left the cemetery, someone else covered the hole in which laid the casket.

*

Oliver was playing with the rim of his glass, where the ice cubes had now fully thawed. He sighed as if he was catching his breath, and then lit a cigarette that he smoked slowly, puff after puff, with his eyes closed.

I was staring at him, in the exact position I was in from the start.

"It really is a strange story," was all he added in between

puffs of smoke.

I was simply fascinated and possibly lost between believing him and wondering if he was making a fool of me. Either way, I could not say anything. I still do not know whether it was the story or the bourbons, but I could not find a single word to say.

Rather than looking for some empty words to say, I joined Oliver and nonchalantly lit a cigarette as well.

I stopped my train of thought and watched the smoke dance around and above our heads.

The pub had started emptying and was now almost silent, creating a very soothing atmosphere.

Like always, it was Oliver who broke the silence to add something to the story he had just finished.

"It was all in his journal apparently. He had written everything like I told you in that journal of his. That is how they found out. The old man he mentions, he is the one who found him. Already dead in the graveyard. Or at least that is what I was told."

"What about the mother?" I do not know what brought this boring detail to my mind but I felt like asking about her. Just imagining the lonely mother of this poor character made me curious. Maybe I was wondering trying to relate to the story, and the thought of my mother hypothetically being left alone after my death struck me.

"I have no idea." He crushed the cigarette in the ash tray and signalled the bartender for another drink. "I imagine she died at some point, the story is quite old, but I can't say for sure."

The mood had become rather strange. Once again, I do not know if it was the many drinks I had in me or Oliver's story, although it would have likely been a bit of both, but I was feeling like something heavy was being put on my shoulders. I was trying really hard not to think much of this story and about Josiah, but mostly, death. But how do you stop thinking about death? It would be the same as to not think about life, or to not think at all. And if you do not think about it, is it not the same as being dead? That was the answer I needed. I was thinking, I was here, I was alive. Of course, one day I would be dead. But that can only happen if you are alive. This conclusion blew all my previous thoughts and doubts and troubles away, like a breath blowing a candle off, or a sweet breeze pushing dark clouds away. And everything was back to normal. Everything was alive. Oliver was still in front of me, slowly drinking his glass of liquor, savouring every second of life we had to the fullest.

I ordered myself a last bourbon as well, and looked at my friend while the bartender lazily filled my glass with ice.

"Yes, it really was a strange story," was all I would bring myself to say.

Mr Basil Livingmore

It was a sunny, but cold 12th of March in the small town of Blackbridge-over-Torrent, with only a few shy clouds tainting an otherwise beautiful sky, where the fading moon remained.

In a small house, at the end of a narrow road, surrounded by a few trees, the rays penetrated the curtains of a bedroom. A very simple, sober bedroom, undecorated. Just a bed, a wardrobe big enough to fit one person's totality of garments, a rug on the ground and a window. On the bed, sat Basil Livingmore, apparently just woken up, looking straight at the white wall in front of him. He knew exactly what day it was, and this brought a smile to his face. Basil Livingmore was a very enthusiastic man when it came to his work. He checked his wristwatch (Basil Livingmore always slept with his wristwatch) to see how much time he had to get ready. The watch hands showed 6.27. It was fairly early, but there was a long day of work ahead.

It did not take him long to get ready: shaven, showered and clad in a few minutes, he was now putting on a heavy trench coat (it was cold as we mentioned), a dark felt hat on top of his head, and an elegant pair of black leather gloves. Fully ready, Basil Livingmore grabbed his case, and after checking the contents (that he had prepared in advance of course, but it never hurt to check), he headed out and locked the door to his house. The long-awaited day of work could now properly start.

*

Blackbridge-over-Torrent was a charming, small and rather unknown town, lost in the middle of a faraway countryside. Only about four hundred people lived there, and it was very far from any big city around. The population's average age was above fifty and for this reason the town was rather quiet and uneventful. No-one seemed to mind however, on the contrary, most of the town's inhabitants enjoyed the peaceful atmosphere and sometimes, when the outside was not too cold, took strolls in the green streets of the town. One thing the town had indeed, was trees. Lots of them. And in between the trees, some animals lived their lives as peacefully as the people did. Squirrels mainly, but more often than not, foxes and does could be seen roaming about.

The town in itself could have been mistaken for a big park, if not for the lovely Victorian houses that sat on the sides of the streets. That day, because it was cold (and also fairly early still) no-one was outside their house. Smoke rose from almost every chimney. People were lazy on Sundays, only Basil Livingmore would be walking around in Blackbridge-over-Torrent on a cold Sunday. And in fact there he was, edging closer and closer to the first house on the street, ready for work.

Before walking the few steps in front of the door, Basil Livingmore checked the house's number and nameplate. It was an old but pretty house, rather large. The curtains, still shut, were concealing the inside. He opened the suitcase, pulled out a notebook and a pen, then he rang the bell.

An old man, still wearing his dressing gown, opened the door after a few seconds, carrying a mug. He didn't seem surprised to see a tall man with a suitcase ringing at his door early on a Sunday morning.

"Ah, Mr Livingmore, we were expecting you. As punctual

17

as ever."

"Good morning, Mr Lewis, glad to hear you remember me. Are you and your Mrs Lewis doing good?"

"Yes, yes, we are just marvellous, thank you. I suppose you would like to collect? I would offer you a cup of tea but I imagine you have a long day of work ahead."

"You are very kind, Mr Lewis, but indeed, I cannot stay."

"Is the fee the same as always?"

Basil Livingmore stopped for a second, and an embarrassed expression appeared on his face. He faked rummaging through the notebook, when in reality he already knew exactly what he was going to tell Mr Lewis.

"In reality, Mr Lewis, how should I put this, I am very sorry but, I am afraid the fee is going to be higher. Last year was, I might say, difficult. I am again very sorry for this."

Mr Lewis did not seem to be disappointed by the news.

"Don't worry too much, Mr Livingmore, you should know that my wife and I are very grateful and satisfied with your work. We all acknowledge your efforts, of course. How much will it be, however?"

Basil Livingmore rubbed his chin while his other hand held the notebook. His suitcase was on the ground, laid against his leg.

"Six hundred forty-eight pounds and twelve pence. I apologise again but, it is out of my hands."

Mr Lewis seemed hesitant for a second, but soon smiled to Basil Livingmore and replied, "Worry not, I will collect the payment."

He went back inside and reappeared on his porch with a large stack of bills.

"I have here six hundred and fifty. I would like you to keep the change. As I said before, we are all very grateful for your work."

"You are too kind, Mr Lewis. Rest assured that you will not regret this. I wish you a very pleasant day, and I will see you next year. Same day same time."

He remained professional and polite in all circumstances. Mr Lewis smiled back and slowly closed the door wishing his visitor 'a fine day and luck with his work.'

Mr Basil Livingmore walked a few steps away from the door and stopped again. He opened back the notebook, to which the pen was attached, and wrote a few words.

Mr and Mrs Lewis – paid.

He then closed the notebook, put it back in the case and started walking to the next house.

*

Basil Livingmore kept going around the small village of Blackbridge-over-Torrent, knocking on the inhabitants' doors, collecting his six hundred and forty-eight pounds and twelve pence from each of them, before carefully recording their name in his notebook, sometimes without a hitch, sometimes having to face the frowns and impolite tone of reticent customers. Some of them seemed disappointed by the fact that the fee had gone up. Others, by the fact that someone was paying a visit early on a Sunday. But everyone payed the fee, without making stories. He however, professional as he was, remained perfectly unfazed and formal with each of them, satisfied that in the end his day of work was progressing successfully. Not that Basil Livingmore enjoyed doing what he did more than anyone else enjoyed doing their own work, but this was his, it was necessary. So he did it and he did it well.

Only two houses were left.

Basil Livingmore rang the bell to the house number 17, on Blacksmith's Road. He waited a few seconds and no one replied. So he rang again.

A strong woman's voice came from behind the closed door. "Who is this?"

Basil Livingmore cleared his throat and replied, speaking somewhat loudly, as no one seemed interested in doing the effort to come to the door.

"Good morning, madam. Basil, Basil Livingmore speaking from Life Tax." Then he added, as if to clarify, "Today is the 12th of March."

No-one replied for a few seconds, then the woman opened the door and appeared. "What do you want from us, Mr Livingmore? Six hundred and twenty one pounds, I assume?" Her tone was defiant, and she didn't seem happy to be bothered by Basil Livingmore on a Sunday morning.

Once again, Basil Livingmore readied himself to deliver the news. He lowered his head and said with apologetic tone,

"Actually, and I am very sorry to say this, the fee has changed this year. It will be six hundred and forty-eight pounds and twelve pence." Basil Livingmore slowly raised his eyes to look at his reticent customer's reaction to the news.

The news seemed to have caused no change in the woman's face, which was already grimacing. Was it because it was too early to be bothered on a Sunday? Was it because paying the fee, no matter which, always put some people in a bad mood? Or was this resident simply not the kind to smile much? The questions quickly passed through Basil Livingmore's mind, but he did not bother trying to find an answer. He was here to do his work after all, not to worry about anything else, and certainly not to befriend his customers.

"Well, Mr Livingmore," the woman began to say, "I will be very honest with you. I am getting pretty tired of giving you such large sums of money every year."

This, was a first for him. People had never complained before. Some showed reluctance, yes, some appeared sceptical, true. But to complain about him doing his work? He did not know how he was to react to this first customer's complaint. He scratched his chin, trying to avoid looking in the woman's eyes.

"I am very sorry that you feel this way, madam, I understand that paying taxes can be a bother. But it is a necessity. I imagine you understand this concept."

The woman did not seem to budge.

"I have been paying your fee for a long time now, Mr Livingmore."

"Yes, it is true. You have been a very punctual and loyal customer for many years. I should thank you for that. But this is a yearly tax. I hope you understand." Basil Livingmore stopped there. To him, no further explanations were needed.

"Well," the woman continued, "let's assume that I decided to not pay your tax this year…" She stopped talking but kept her eyes straight on Basil Livingmore's face, as to challenge him.

"What happens next?"

Basil Livingmore finally raised his head and stared back in his reticent customer's eyes, his face back to a professional complete lack of expression.

"I must admit, it has never happened before," he replied, "so I cannot say with certainty what will actually happen. What I can tell for sure however, is that you will no longer benefit from my services."

The woman crossed her arms, still staring at the strange

looking man, bothering her on a Sunday morning about wanting her money.

"Your services? Your 'Life Tax' services?"

"Precisely, madam. Life Tax will no longer offer you their services, if you do not pay the fee. That is how Life Tax works." Again, Basil Livingmore explained everything in his very plain tone, as if stating the evident.

"Well, Mr, I would tell you it has been a pleasure chatting with you, but it would be a lie."

Basil Livingmore looked, without letting his face express his mixed feelings about what was happening, as the woman slowly returned inside her house.

"I no longer wish to pay for your so-called 'services'," were her final words, and then she closed the door behind her.

It took several seconds for Basil Livingmore to realise what had just happened. He could not remember how many years he had been doing this work for (they were many that was certain), and never, not once in his career had a customer so rudely announced him that his services were not appreciated. True, the fee had gone up several times since he had started working, he understood that, but nevertheless, the situation had confused him. Resigned, however, and professional as always, he opened his leather case, extracted the pen and notebook and proceeded to write down:

17, Blacksmith's Road – not payed.

The hands on his watch were now showing 2.38. Time had flown, but the day of hard work was now nearing its end. After the rather unpleasant experience, Basil Livingmore walked to the last house left still with mixed emotions. Quickly enough however, he returned to his professional state, and prepared to collect the remaining fee, before finally heading home.

*

On the 13th of March, the small population of Blackbridge-over-Torrent woke up, all around the same time. It was a Monday, but given the age average in the town, this was not the reason everyone was agitating around the usually quiet streets.

Half of the town's men and women had all gathered in front of the remains of an old Victorian house, the blackened, still smoking remains of the house situated on 17, Blacksmith's Road. No-one could quite tell how and when it had happened, but it was clear that overnight the small house at the end of the street, had simply caught fire. Everyone knew who was the owner of the house, because everyone in town knew each other. Old Mrs Gilmour, widowed, living alone at 17 Blacksmith's Road. Needless to say, no effort was made into finding her. It was more than evident to everyone around that the silent and sudden fire that no-one seemed to have noticed, had taken her along with the majority of her home.

The people who had gathered exchanged a few words only. Someone said, "Tragic is it not?" Someone else reminded others how she would always say good morning or good evening when you passed her by, and some other pointed out that it was curious how a fire would breakout with no-one noticing, but there was nothing that could have been done, and such was life sometimes.

After this exchange of banalities, everyone slowly returned to their own preoccupations and soon enough, old Mrs Gilmour was forgotten.

A few days later, a tombstone with her name was added to the nearby graveyard, and whatever the fire had left of the house was removed.

After that happened, and after it had become a fading memory, spring, in the quiet town of Blackbridge-over-Torrent went on, as uneventful as it always had.

Olive Leaf

The night everything began, I was lying in bed naked, next to Rachel, a girl I had met a few months before. That night, she had needed someone to feel close to, even if just for a little while. As for me, I had needed something to break the routine and the boredom of a long week. She seemed to like me enough and I did not particularly dislike her, our needs coincided, and we both happened to be at the same event that night, out drinking, with mutual friends of ours.

She was resting her head on my arm, we were enjoying the particular atmosphere of that night and the warmth of our bodies, in silence. Only the unique sound of raindrops tapping against the window could be heard.

By the time we had come back to her place (she had insisted that we do), a heavy rain had already started to fall down. It had been about two hours since it had started. It was normal for a wintery evening in London, but it still had managed to catch us by surprise. It had not let off at all, had kept pouring and pouring throughout the night and did not seem like it was going to stop soon. We just kept laying there, resting, with this appeasing sound as our only companion. It was already a heavy and menacing storm, but back then, I had obviously no idea what was about to happen.

Rachel was gently caressing my chest, still resting her head on me, with her eyes half shut. She broke the silence.

"Can you imagine if this rain never stopped?" she said this

in between chuckles.

I smiled, amused before replying.

"You mean like in the Bible?" Because such is my humour.

"Yes, like in the Bible." She seemed to go along with it.

A lighting strike lit up the room for a second, and the loud sound of thunder followed. It may have been my imagination, but I think it is at that exact moment that the rain started falling even harder than before, as if our short conversation had somehow summoned what was waiting for us.

I closed my eyes, appreciating this soothing atmosphere (at the time, rainy nights were truly a blissful enjoyment of mine, and perhaps what I loved the most about living in London), as well as the warmth of the girl beside me. She curled up even closer, and we both fell asleep.

I was woken up in the middle of my night by yet another loud thunder clap. This time, I am sure of it, the rain had started coming down harder than what I had ever witnessed before. I noticed that Rachel was still sound asleep. Not even the loud sound of thunder, not even the battering rain, almost threatening to crush the window, could seem to wake her up.

I got up from the bed, careful as to not wake her up, walked slowly to the window and peeked between the curtains. I wanted to get a glimpse of the chaos outside. And chaos it was. Rain, unrelenting cold rain was coming down on the streets and roofs of London. The lampposts' faint light was barely filtering through the deluge. I was reminded of my Bible joke earlier, and realised that now, it seemed like God's anger, truly was descending upon us. I stayed there a few minutes, hypnotised by the Sublime of this torrential rain beating down on the mighty English city. It felt, to me, as a modern Titanomachy.

I began wondering for how long the sky would keep on

raining down, and what would the city look like afterwards. I was hoping I would be able to leave early the next morning, leave this almost stranger to her life and return to mine like nothing had happened, but while I was watching this spectacular display of a rainstorm, it was difficult to see myself casually walking the streets of London. Resigned and realising my fatigue was taking over again, I returned to the bed, and listening to Rachel's slow, calm breathing, I fell asleep again.

When I woke up again the next morning, I noticed first of all that my head was pounding and spinning a little. I realised the alcohol from the night before had not worn off entirely. Secondly, I noticed that the bed was now empty, which did not worry me too much, it was well past seven already. Finally, I noticed the light from outside was barely visible through the curtains, which meant that the sun was still covered by dark clouds. Most importantly, I noticed that the sound of the rain was still as loud as it had been all night. Although, London is famous for its wet weather, I was starting to find it unusual for such a mighty rainstorm to persevere as this one was. I began to ask myself if there was a possibility that the Thames might overflow, which had never happened in the years I had been living in the capital. If it were to happen, it would undoubtedly be a catastrophe. Would the whole city be on hold? Would people be allowed to roam the busy streets like they always did? I quickly brushed off these questions, convincing myself that the rain would stop at some point and that life was, after all, still following its natural course. My thinking was also interrupted by Rachel, who entered the room with a mug in each hand.

"Good morning! Coffee?"

Her tone was jovial and she was smiling.

"Sure, that's very sweet of you," I replied, as I took the mug she was handing me. She sat down on the bed, keeping her happy expression as she looked at me, and we sipped the warm coffee in silence for a few seconds.

"You look in a good mood. Are you always a morning person?" I asked.

"I just got a call from work. The trains are not running, so no shift today," she replied. The idea of not going to work seemed to please her.

Then, it hit me. Trains not running. This rain had managed to put one business, possibly multiple that I did not know of, on hiatus, and had stopped the trains from running, after just a night. By London standards, that was almost beyond belief. The train system is the heartbeat of this city. If the trains don't work, it means half of the city at least is held hostage. This should have rang an alarm bell, but back then I was too hazy, tired and yet reasonable to worry, and I accepted that these sort of things just happen sometimes.

"That is a great news. Resting today then I assume." I resumed sipping my coffee.

"Yes, most likely, with this rain and no trains, there is not much else I could do today anyways. I will stay in, I think."

I was trying to think fast. Was I going to be able to leave soon? I could walk the way back to my flat of course and my work did not require me to show up to any office, but this rain was beginning to feel really threatening. I was hoping Rachel would not mind me waiting until the rain let off. She anticipated my question.

"Were you planning on going back soon? It looks like it would be complicated, if not dangerous to go out there for now."

"I am not sure. It will stop eventually, won't it?"

"I have no idea. I have not checked the weather or the news

yet."

"Well, I will have to go at some point. I do not plan on being in your hair on your rest day."

"You can wait for it to quiet down, I really don't mind," she reassured me, still with a cheerful expression.

It was the answer I was hoping for. Although I would usually not stick around in the flat of someone I had only and just spent a night with, this felt like special circumstances. And I think that at the time I felt that something about Rachel and the atmosphere were different. For some reason, there was no uneasiness about sticking around longer than needed. It did not feel wrong and I did not feel like I had to get out of here as quickly as possible. I was enjoying a coffee and small talk with a friendly person, not a close friend of course but still, surrounded by the sound of rain crushing down outside.

After the coffee was finished, we both set on to find an occupation as we waited for the rain to pass. Rachel decided this was the perfect occasion to tidy up her flat a little, and pointed me towards the bookshelf in her room. She knew I loved reading and there was nothing else I could do for the time being. I did think of offering to help with the tidying up, but it occurred to me it might have been somewhat awkward, and I wanted to avoid that.

I sat down on the small sofa facing the bed and flipped around a few pages of a novel I had picked from the shelf.

But I could not focus. The rain kept falling and falling incessantly and the sound of this rain was starting to irritate me. My mind started racing. What if it did never stop? What if, by some random chance, we were experiencing a natural phenomenon of catastrophic proportions, the likes of which had not happened in years? Was I stuck in an almost stranger's flat for an indefinite amount of time? It felt weird thinking that after just half a day of rain. That was more than regular occurrence, but something about this particular rain, the intensity, the heaviness, the unnatural loudness of this rain, that left me unable to keep my mind at peace.

I closed the novel and left it on the coffee table in front of me, before getting up and walking to the window. I needed to see this storm again. London was barely visible. The roofs, the streets, the trees and the buildings, were all hidden behind a curtain of falling water, and a thin fog had begun to settle as well. The roads, usually busy with people and cars alike, were empty and quiet. Only the ruckus of the rain could be heard. It felt unnatural, and of course, though I could not fully wrap my head around it yet at the time, it most definitely was.

I could hear Rachel from the kitchen, humming a tune I did not know, while she was still apparently tidying up, and it pulled me out of my reverie. I decided I would help her and maybe try to small talk, in a while at least. I was after all her guest, she had kindly allowed me to wait in her flat and I was feeling restless reading by myself.

It occurred to me at that time that despite the fact that we had mutual friends and that we had spent a night together, I knew very little about her. I thought that helping her cleaning up whatever it is she was working on, and exchange a few words, would sort of humanise the relationship a little. I picked up the novel again and read for another hour or so.

I finished the first few chapters of the novel and closed it again before stretching. Not much time had passed, but I was not captivated enough by the book. Rachel had not come back in the room yet.

I walked out of the room and into the kitchen, and it took me a few seconds to realise what was happening. Rachel was not moving. She was standing in front of her sink, her back turned at me, facing the window. I wondered what she could possibly be looking at, since the glass pane was entirely covered in a mixture of raindrops and cold fog, the outside world had become invisible from the flat. The sky was evidently still hidden by thick grey clouds, and the rain continued to fall incessantly, its sound interrupted only once in a while, by the loud cracks of thunder, hovering above London. I was hesitating to make my presence known; she seemed lost in thought and completely focused at the same time. I realised I had unconsciously stopped breathing, as if trying to conceal myself. She seemed to finally come to her senses and turned around to look at me.

"Is everything all right?" she asked me.

"Yes, I was just wondering if you really didn't need any help. I really don't mind giving you a hand, I don't have much else to do after all."

She paused. She was looking at me with an expression I had not seen from her yet. It was no longer the joyful, tune-humming girl I had woken up to. For some reason, Rachel was not smiling, and her eyes were not sparkling at all. They seemed dark and confused.

"It's OK, really, I am basically done cleaning here," she said, as she slowly walked away from the sink. She brushed past me to head back into the main room, and I noticed she gently rubbed her eyes as she did.

I followed her and sat back in the sofa, as she approached the bedside table, on which stood a small radio. She switched on the radio and as she searched for the right frequency, telling me that she wanted to hear the news.

"Surely, there will be something about the weather. Even for

London this is not common."

I was glad that she mentioned this, I had thought I was being paranoid, but no. This rain, this thunder, these litres and litres of water falling down and keeping me prisoner in an almost stranger's flat, was not a normal occurrence. She stopped on a certain frequency and we caught the speaker in the middle of his speech.

As we expected, the rain was going to keep falling, and there was for now no way to say when it would stop. He explained that meteorologists could not explain how or why it had started to rain this hard and that, as we had now understood, we were experiencing a very rare phenomenon. Then came the part I feared. Trains in London were still not running, as many stations were under high alert of being flooded. Besides that, the storm had overnight, as you would expect it to, produced some heavy damage: trees had fallen of course, and walking the streets for now had been deemed to be 'dangerous'. Londoners were requested to stay inside and not go out under any circumstance, until the rain and wind calmed down. That announcement had condemned me. I could not leave. Who knew when the storm would stop? No one. I was stuck, and I had no way to know for how long.

Rachel turned off the radio after the announcement had finished. She turned her head towards the window and her eyes got lost looking at the storm. Her cheerfulness of the morning now seemed like a distant memory, so much that I wondered if I had imagined it. Her face displayed complete lack of expression, if not a hint of sadness. She caught me by surprise, and while still staring blankly at the dark clouds outside, said to me, "How long have we known each other?"

The tone in which she was speaking seemed so strange. Far

away, there was something cold in her voice.

I asked myself, why that question would come up.

"Half year… seven months maybe?" I was confused but did not know what else to answer, other than an honest fact.

"Why are you lying?"

I was struck by that reply. Was I lying? I was convinced I was correct, and I still did not understand where this awkward conversation was going, or where it was coming from.

I had to say something, Rachel was now looking at me and definitely expecting a reply, her expression was turning from blank to what seemed a mixture of sadness and anger.

I tried to open my mouth and come up with something to say, but the words would not come out. I was saved by yet another deafening crack of thunder breaking this heavy silence, and a strong gush of wind blasting the window open. The rain, falling harder than it even had until now, and the wind howling, entered the room. But Rachel did not budge, she was unbothered by the chaos threatening her room. This girl stood there by the window, staring at me. And tears, started falling down her cheeks. I thought they were raindrops at first but no. Rachel was crying. I could not move, the storm was now inside the flat and she would not move to close the window. A few seconds passed and taken aback I rushed to the window and closed it myself. Rachel remained immobile, with tears slowly crawling down her face.

"Seven years," she said, now facing the floor, weeping with eyes closed. "We have known each other for seven years. How can you not remember?"

She kept crying and crying, trying to stop her sobs coming out, and resumed, "I was your friend for seven years, and one day you left."

32

I, of course still could not believe what was happening. This girl I was sure, was someone I had met recently. Bewildered, I kept looking her like she was insane.

"One day you left and forgot about me. I tried to reach you, but you never replied," she continued, between sobs and tears.

Was that possible? It could not be. But for some reason, I knew she was telling the truth.

I remained speechless. What could I have possibly said after all? I was certain I had never known her before, and she was certain we had been friends for seven years before I disappeared from her life. And we were both telling the truth.

Her crying became stronger and she sat on the bed. My eyes were suddenly drawn to the storm outside, relentless. I could not face this crying girl in front of me.

Rachel added nothing else and kept crying while sitting on her bed.

Where had these seven years gone? Did my brain, my heart, my soul, did they really erase this person from memory? Had Rachel really been a part of my life that had mysteriously disappeared? I now realise that this is not what had happened, it was nothing mysterious. One day, I left, and forgot about her. I had decided she had never existed. And my mind had gradually erased her from existence. I do not know the reason, I do not understand how it might even be possible, but I know that it happened. Rachel's tears and desperate tone were as true as my memories.

I sat down on the floor my eyes fixed on the window and lost in my thoughts, my chest hurting. The rain kept battering on the glass and the storm kept its concerto of sound and lights.

Rachel's sobs became quieter and her breathing took a calmer, regular breathing. In the dark of the room, now lying in bed, she had slowly cried herself to sleep.

I remained there, broken, confused and choked by a feeling I could never describe. The feeling I had done something terrible, irreparable and that I had never had control over.

Minutes passed at first, then hours. I stayed sitting on the floor completely lost through the whole afternoon, the evening and then the night. Rachel was sound sleep.

By daybreak, I was pulled out of my trance. The first, shy rays of the sun filtered from under the curtain and that is when I realised. Without me knowing when, and how, the rain had stopped. The sky was now quiet and the clouds, began letting the sun shine upon London again. I got on my feet, made sure to quietly leave the room, avoiding to wake up the stranger lying in her bed, I grabbed my jacket from the hanger on the door. Opening the door to leave the building, I asked myself if everything was real. Pushing these thoughts away, I began walking the streets of the city after the storm. The pavement was sparkling here and there from the rays reflecting in the puddles, and the trees, deprived of their leaves, remained still, as the wind was no longer blowing. I walked.

Needless to say, I never saw her again.

The Odd One Out

I was the last one to move in the five-bedroom flat that the whole group inhabited. At least the last one from that group. We were all former students in the same promotion, and had managed to stick together through our evolution towards true adulthood. There were only four of us, but Michael, the most responsible and experienced member of our group (I would use the word leader to describe Michael's place in the group, but he never quite saw himself as that, or attempted to behave in such a way), had managed to obtain a lease for a good price in this lovely five bedrooms flat for all of us to live in. Michael's parents were somewhat close to the landlord as he had explained to us, and the flat was appealing, spacious and well placed within the city. Everyone including me were more than satisfied with living together in this flat for the complicated times that were lying ahead, so we were very grateful, and we all made sure we worked hard to make life go as smoothly as possible in the flat and the group. The fifth bedroom, the second one on the second floor and coincidentally the one in front of mine, would simply remain empty. The flat had everything else we needed and wanted: a large kitchen and a comfortable living space on the ground floor, three bedrooms and the large bathroom on the first floor, and the last two rooms with a smaller bathroom on the second. We had agreed when seeing the flat for the first time that I would live by myself on the second floor, rather than splitting the group in two groups of two: it was not because they were ostracising me although it might be how I am making it sound, the reality is that although I was very fond of the people in our group, I enjoyed quiet and solitude more than the other three. They understood that and were more than pleased to go with my request. Incidentally, it meant that I would be living in a room that was slightly larger than the ones on the first floor, but again this did not seem to bother anyone either. In addition to Michael and I, the group also had two girls, Ellie and Sophie. The three of them worked miscellaneous jobs, at the bottom of the hierarchy of a small law firm. I on the other hand, had started working as an assistant to the editor of an independent magazine. Our schedules were busy, and we only had time to spend together in the flat late in the evening. I would sometimes join the other three for a drink or a chat, and everything went smoothly. Although we all got along however, I was more than aware than all three of them were closer to each other than I was to any of them. It did not bother me however, socialising had never been either my forte or something I really cared for in the first place. I was friends with them, close enough to share a flat and spend time as a group, and that was more than enough. I had never felt the need, or a spontaneous feeling to want to connect with them any more than I already was.

The first weeks went by without a hitch, I was slowly beginning to settle in my work. Most days, I did not even need to leave the flat to do it. I started to enjoy the quiet lifestyle that being alone on the top floor provided. Having an empty bedroom in front of mine did not feel as gloomy and ominous as I thought it would at first.

Sometimes, while walking around the flat for the occasional bathroom or coffee break during the day, I would quietly pry the door of the empty bedroom open, and take a glance inside. I do not know why I did it, but I did. I do not know if I was expecting either to find it suddenly inhabited by a stranger, or realise that the furniture and decoration had changed. The more times I found myself looking inside that bedroom, the more I started printing in my mind what it exactly looked like. It was always dark of course, I never bothered switching the lights on and a heavy curtain covered the large window of the room. Due to the lack of a tenant, the fifth bedroom was spartan looking, to say the least. A queen-size bed without any linen, a small wooden desk in the corner with a chair, a few simple shelves and a wardrobe. Nothing more. There were no rugs, nothing to cover the white walls.

I began appreciating the aesthetic of that empty, silent bedroom, a different comfort than my brighter, slightly more decorated bedroom. A recurrent peeking into the fifth bedroom quickly became a strange, but pleasant habit, a moment of pause in my busy work days, between my own bedroom and the rest of the flat I lived in.

I remember asking Michael one day, as we were seating in the kitchen after he had come back from his office, if there was a chance that the fifth bedroom would be occupied at some point, and he told me he had no idea. The landlord only told him that the four of us could occupy the flat and that they had not mentioned looking for a fifth one. It reassured me, as the current situation satisfied me. But of course, it was more than likely that this would actually change.

An empty bedroom in a flat in London, what is more at a reasonable price, was bound to attract interest.

*

Winter had finally started settling in. The city grew colder, the trees got more and more barren, and the dark came earlier each day. It was in this period that I truly appreciated the fact that I could stay at home most of the time, even more so than usual.

One such evening, I was sitting at my desk finishing writing an article requested by my editor. With my record player on, I lazily listened to a disc I had randomly picked from my shelf. Paul Anka's *Put Your Head on My Shoulder* was playing, as I watched the scene outside my window. The lamp-posts in the streets shone bright, the low humming of cars occasionally came and went. It was a truly appeasing scene.

My three flat-mates were all out working from their office, as almost every day. With the flat to myself, I decided to get up and go make myself some coffee. Maybe sit in the living room with a book for a while, for a change of scenery and a break.

I climbed down the stairs, but as I entered the kitchen, the noise of keys rustling, came from the front door. Someone I had never seen before, a man in a long brown coat, carrying a backpack, entered the flat and closed the door. I was too surprised to react at first and remained there standing in the corner of the kitchen.

The man was tall, almost as tall as I was, and had long brown hair, tied in a bun. The first thing he did as he entered, was unravel the long red scarf around his neck. This revealed a well taken care of moustache that made it difficult to guess his age. He could have been anywhere between his early twenties and late thirties. He folded his scarf and placed his backpack on the floor, then started looking around the flat, and finally, noticed me.

"Hello," he said, slightly bowing his head to me. The man had a subtle foreign accent that I could not place immediately. "I'm Tom, the new tenant."

It took me a few seconds to take in what was happening. A new tenant. I had not been warned about it. Neither Michael nor the landlord had told me that the fifth bedroom had now a tenant.

"Hello, Tom, pleasure to meet you," I replied, as I walked towards him. I held out my hand to greet him formally, and he seemed to accept it gratefully. He had a strong handshake, and he was smiling. A comforting smile, one that showed he truly was pleased to be here and to be accepted as a newcomer.

"The others are all out, but I'm working from home," I started. "I can show you around the flat if you'd like."

"Please, I would be very grateful."

The more he spoke, the more evident his accent became. Tom was French. There was of course, nothing unusual about a Frenchman living in London, but I was curious. What did he do? Had he been in London for long? Did he know any of my other flat-mates? I had so many questions, but I did not want to seem rude, so I kept them to myself. Besides, it was really not my thing to ask questions and pry into the life of people I had just met. If Tom was going to be living with us, on my floor nonetheless, since there was the last empty room, we were going to get to know each other at some point.

I showed Tom around the whole flat. There was not that much to see: the ground floor's kitchen and living room, the bathrooms and finally, I took him to the last bedroom.

He examined it thoroughly, as I stayed silent outside the door.

"I think I will be more than fine here, thank you for showing me around."

"Of course."

I thought about asking him what he did as a job and where he was from, but decided against it. For now, I would let him settle in. I went back to my room after telling him to knock on my door if he had any questions.

That evening, I focused on finishing my manuscript in time, and made sure my supervisor was satisfied. Since I managed, it meant I had the rest of the week to myself. I would enjoy the winter atmosphere, some background music, a cup of warm coffee and most importantly a good book. Already savouring the peaceful days of rest to come. I went to browse my bookshelf in search of something I had not read yet. I stood there for around five minutes, looking, reading the titles, the authors, and pondering, before finally realising that nothing appealed to me. There was not a single book that called to me to take it. I decided it had been a while since I had visited a bookshop. Trips to the London bookshops were one of my favourite distractions, so I left my room ready to fight the cold. As I got out, I almost caught myself about to peek in the no longer empty bedroom, instinctively.

The door was not closed, and I could hear the faint music coming from within the room. I was surprised to realise my new neighbour was listening to *Be My Baby* by the Ronettes. Another fan of oldies was now in the flat. I thought to myself, *It would likely become a conversation topic if we ever ended up having a talk. It wouldn't be too bad, socialising over good music taste.* I decided to not linger in front of his room and went downstairs to leave, in search of a book to keep me busy.

It was still early, perhaps six in the evening, but the sun had already set completely. London was lit up by street lamps, a bitter cold breeze forced me to bury my face inside the heavy scarf around my neck. There were people and cars passing all around me, but I was not paying attention to my surrounding, too busy keeping my head down towards the pavement and wandering inside my own thoughts. Who was the quiet new neighbour of mine? Why was I not warned of his arrival? Were my other flat-mates aware of our fifth tenant? From time to time, a noise, or a smell, coming from the bright shops along the road pulled me out of my thinking, reminding me where I was going. I decided that Michael had been most likely notified of Tom's arrival and he had simply forgot to mention it, given how little time we had seen each other in the recent days, both busy with our new lives. After all, our flat had five rooms. For there to be five tenants was, ultimately, the most natural thing in the world.

*

I returned to the flat an hour later with a copy of Woolf's *To the Lighthouse* under my arm. It was as often, very quiet. The others were most likely still at work or on their way to drink with colleagues before the weekend. I had of course no real need for such plans and was simply thinking about sitting somewhere with a warm coffee and my new book, to enjoy the days of rest ahead. My troubling thinking had vanished, and the quiet flat was not unsettling in the least. Seeing the new flat-mate's coat untouched on the hanger near the door however, brought back the questions I had about the situation. It prompted me to check on him before locking myself in my room. I climbed up the stairs silently, and realised the music from the fifth bedroom was still somewhat audible. I immediately recognised Presley's *Blue Suede Shoes*. Another oldie, and a good one too. The door was still open, although just slightly.

I knocked on the door, and before I could announce myself, I heard Tom's voice telling me to come in. The voice sounded clear and loud, but it seemed to come from a distance. I realised why as I pushed the door. The curtain was open, and outside the window was Tom, sitting on the balcony of his room. As I had never entered the room before, only peeked inside from the door, it had never occurred to me that one of the bedrooms even had a balcony. After all, it was the only room in the flat with a balcony.

Tom looked at me and showed the chair beside him with his hand. I gave a smile and sat next to him. The view from that balcony was nothing special. A few meters below was the street, a narrow one with a few trees and lampposts. Opposite Tom's room was the large complex, with most of the windows' curtains pulled in front of them. The wind was starting to pick up, and we both remained seated for a while saying nothing, until Tom grabbed a cigarette from the pack laying on a small garden table in front of us, and offered me one. I accepted it and waited for him to light it. As I took the lighter from his fingers, he puffed out the smoke, and said, "I am sorry, I don't really do small talk. But if you have any questions feel free to ask."

It surprised me, but I think I understood what he meant. For the longest of times, the reason I did not attempt to get close to people or even start conversations with strangers, was also because I despised small talk. The weather, the 'what do you do for a living' and other shallow, impersonal questions had always annoyed me. If the conversation is not interesting and the relationship is artificial, then where is the point, I would think to myself.

It took me a moment to decide what I should have asked him. I did not want to annoy my new encounter with the basic questions he was most likely trying to avoid, so while I puffed away at his kindly offered cigarette, I pondered. He did not seem to mind the silence at all. Then I gave up looking for a deep question to ask and decided that since I knew nothing about him but his name, perhaps some simple questions were a good start.

"What brings you to London?"

That was not the most interesting of questions I suppose, but I was curious. I hoped he would not be offended by the simplicity of it. Or maybe the opposite, perhaps was I being too intrusive from the get-go?

Tom did not reply. He crushed his cigarette butt in the ashtray in front of him, and stared at the complex opposite of us. But his eyes seemed like they were looking through the building, aiming for something much further away.

"This place is… unexpectedly quiet. Peaceful," he started. "Are you often by yourself here?"

I did not expect him to be the one asking instead of answering my question. But I did not want to make him uncomfortable.

"I suppose so. I'm the only one who works from home, I don't go out that much."

"I see," was all he added.

I waited a little for him to see if he would ask another questions.

"I like being by myself," he said, "but sometimes, you need others."

He certainly spoke in an interesting way. His French accent, I must say, added a certain something to his speech that I could not describe accurately. It was a feeling between wise and eerie.

He was opening up to some extent, so I suddenly found it easier to reply to him. I thought I would open up as well to him.

"I find it difficult to trust others to be honest." I realised my cigarette was no longer lit. "That's probably why I prefer staying this way." That is when I realised how paradoxical that sounded. What I said was true, but for some reason, talking about that to him, a man I had just met and of whom I knew nothing of, felt natural to me.

"I understand." He got up from his chair and I did the same. I did not want to impose more on him.

"No one really understands you. Who you really are, I mean," he continued, without looking at me.

"Because you feel like you are by yourself, even around people, you choose to be by yourself at all times." I really did not expect him to go that deep in his first conversation with a stranger. I did not know how to reply. So I did not. Filling the silence is not always necessary, I figured. And he was right about how I felt. I imagine he felt the same way. Sometimes, it is simpler to relate to someone you barely know, than to your oldest acquaintances, for some strange reason.

I realised then that his music had stopped playing. Tom was standing in the room, doing nothing in particular. As I walked towards the door to leave, still a little lost in my thoughts, digesting our short conversation, I turned around and told him that I liked his music taste.

"I know," he answered, and smiled, once again.

I returned to my room and sat back at the desk, still thinking. It was late at this point and the bedroom was dark. The flat was now more silent than ever.

*

I was woken up by the sound of the door downstairs closing. I heard Michael's voice humming a tune to himself, so I slowly walked to the kitchen to welcome him.

"Good evening!" He was always cheerful when coming back from work.

44

"Did you meet Tom already?" I asked. I wanted to know if he had at least been warned of our newest flat-mate.

He looked at me with confusion on his face.

"Who is that?"

"Our new flat-mate. Didn't the landlord tell you?"

He looked more and more puzzled. He took off his coat and hung it next to the door. Tom's coat however was no longer there. Nor was his scarf.

I did not know what to say. Tom may have gone outside without me knowing, while I was asleep, but it did not feel right somehow. Michael had not been warned that someone else was moving in.

"Are you still asleep?" he asked me, chuckling.

I felt a chill. Something with the atmosphere was wrong. Something with the words coming out of my mouth felt wrong.

"There's a new flat-mate," I started, "living in the room next to mine."

"OK, that is strange."

I suddenly felt lightheaded. That feeling that 'something was wrong' became unbearable, it was crushing me slowly, but I simply could not put my finger on what it was. The world felt like a shattered mirror. Every piece was there, but at the same time it was not the way it is supposed to be.

I rushed up the stairs and stopped in front of the door in front of my bedroom's. The air was heavy, it was hard to breathe. Or perhaps I was holding my breath; I cannot be sure.

I knocked and heard no answers. Michael had followed me up the stairs at a leisurely pace.

"Is everything all right?" I heard him say.

My hand was shaking a little, as I forced myself to turn the knob and open that door. But the door was not actually closed.

45

There was of course, no music. In fact there was no record player any more. The curtains were pulled, the room was dark. The walls naked. It was as empty and spartan as it always had been. No trace of clothing, bags. No trace that a person had ever set foot inside the room.

At that moment, every piece of that shattered mirror fell from the frame.

At that moment, I felt lonelier than I ever had in my entire existence.